Book Club Edition

First American Edition

Copyright © 1977

All rights reserved under International and Pan-American Copyright Conventions.
Published in the United States by Random House, Inc., New York,
and simultaneously in Canada by Random House of Canada Limited, Toronto.
Originally published in Denmark as Løven Lambert by Gutenberghus Bladene, Copenhagen.

ISBN: 0-394-83839-4   ISBN: 0-394-93839-9 (lib. bdg.)

Manufactured in the United States of America 1 2 3 4 5 6 7 8 9 0
A B C D E F G H I J K
8

WALT DISNEY'S

Lambert
the Sheepish
Lion

Random House New York

Mr. Stork was having
a busy night.
He had to deliver
bundles of babies
to all kinds of places.

As he flew over the trees,
Mr. Stork was glad he had just
one bundle left.

Early in the morning Mr. Stork
came at last to a sheep meadow.
The sheep were still asleep.
"This must be the place," thought
Mr. Stork.
The address on his bundle said:

BABY LAMBS.

DELIVER TO SHEEP MEADOW.

Mr. Stork flipped his wings up
and swooped down.
He made a perfect landing.

Six mother sheep were waiting in a row.

Out of the sack tumbled five baby lambs.
"Here is your home," Mr. Stork told them.

"Just pick out the sheep you like best,"
said Mr. Stork. "She will be your mother."
Soon each little lamb had found a warm,
woolly mother.

But there was
one mother sheep
who had no little lamb.
A tear fell
from her eye.

"Oh dear," said Mr. Stork. "I thought
I had enough lambs to go around."
He picked up the sack and shook it.
Out tumbled one more baby!

"YOU don't look like a lamb," said
the stork.

He took out his spectacles and
checked his order book.

"Why, you must be
Lambert, the lion cub,"
he said.

But by then Lambert had found
the lonely mother sheep.

Lambert snuggled up beside her.
She did not look lonely any more.

"Excuse me, Mrs. Sheep," said
Mr. Stork. "There is a mistake.
That is a lion cub!
"I will just take him away.
He will not bother you again."

Mrs. Sheep was furious.
Lambert was her baby.
No one was going to take him away.

Mrs. Sheep rammed her big head—POW!
—right into Mr. Stork.

Mr. Stork flew into the air, spectacles
and all.

That was enough for him.

He got out of that sheep meadow just
as fast as he could flap his wings.

"Silly old stork!" said Mrs. Sheep
as she licked Lambert's little mane.
Lambert purred like a kitten.

The other mothers
were licking their
babies, too.

"Now run and play,"
said Mrs. Sheep.

And off went Lambert.

Lambert watched the lambs
playing on the grass.
They were having fun.

They jumped and leaped
about on stiff, wobbly legs.
"Baaa, baaa!" they said.

Lambert opened his mouth to say BAAA.
He wanted to play too.
But all that came out was a great
big MEOW!

The lambs thought that MEOW was a very
funny sound for a lamb to make.

They laughed and laughed at Lambert.

"How silly he looks!" said one lamb.
"His feet are too big."

"His tail is too long," said another.

Poor Lambert! He felt very sad.

His feet WERE too big.

His tail WAS too long.

He was the silliest-looking lamb
in the meadow.

Lambert's mother came to comfort him.
"Never mind, dear," she said. "Just
play with the lambs and do what they do.
You will grow up to be a fine sheep."

Lambert felt much better.

He went off to play.

But every time Lambert
tried to leap like a lamb,
he tripped over his big feet...

...and landed on his head.

And every time he tried to butt
heads with another lamb, the lamb
would ram—POW!—into him.

After a while, Lambert had a very
sore head.

"Never mind, dear,"
said his mother. "You
are growing faster than
all the others."

Lambert WAS growing fast!

Every day he was getting bigger and
BIGGER and BIGGER!

But as Lambert grew bigger,
he grew more and more sheepish.

He never acted angry when the young sheep laughed at him.

Lambert just grinned his sheepish grin and pretended not to care.

But Lambert DID care.

He was tired of being butted.

He was tired of looking silly.

Most of all, he was tired
of being different.

One night, while all the sheep were
sleeping, Lambert woke up.

He pricked up his ears.

A wolf was creeping slowly toward
the sheep meadow!

It was growling a mean, hungry growl!

The wolf was coming
to get the sheep.
Lambert was terrified.

Lambert hid behind his mother.
He did not feel brave enough
to fight that wolf.

But the sheep were not brave either.
They were as sheepish as sheep can be.
When they heard the wolf coming,
all the sheep ran into the woods.
They hid behind the trees.
Lambert was surprised.

Even his mother, who had butted
Mr. Stork, was trembling now.

Suddenly something went SNAP inside
Lambert's head.

He forgot how sheepish he had become.

He forgot that he was afraid.

He even forgot to try and say BAAA.

He opened his mouth and ROAR-R-RED!
Then he dashed after the wolf.

But Lambert did not forget EVERYTHING
he had learned in the sheep meadow.

He rammed his big head—POW!—
right into the wolf.

The wolf went flying over the edge
of a cliff.

In all his sheep-hunting days,
the wolf had never before seen a lion.

But one lion was
enough for him.
The wolf never
bothered the sheep again.

All the sheep gathered around Lambert.
They were not laughing at him now.
Lambert was a great hero!
"My Lambert is a mighty lion," said
Mrs. Sheep. "Did you hear him roar?"
Lambert purred happily.
But it was a mighty purr—
a lion's purr.